Oxford
Progressive
English Readers

TALES FROM THE ARABIAN NIGHTS

The *Oxford Progressive English Readers* series provides a wide range of reading for learners of English.

Each book in the series has been written to follow the strict guidelines of a syllabus, wordlist and structure list. The texts are graded according to these guidelines; Grade 1 at a 1,400 word level, Grade 2 at a 2,100 word level, Grade 3 at a 3,100 word level, Grade 4 at a 3,700 word level and Grade 5 at a 5,000 word level.

The latest methods of text analysis, using specially designed software, ensure that readability is carefully controlled at every level. Any new words which are vital to the mood and style of the story are explained within the text, and reoccur throughout for maximum reinforcement. New language items are also clarified by attractive illustrations.

Each book has a short section containing carefully graded exercises and controlled activities, which test both global and specific understanding.

Tales From
The Arabian Nights

Edited by David Foulds

Hong Kong
Oxford University Press
Oxford

Oxford University Press

Oxford   New York
Athens   Auckland   Bangkok   Bombay
Calcutta   Cape Town   Dar es Salaam   Delhi
Florence   Hong Kong   Istanbul   Karachi
Kuala Lumpur   Madras   Madrid   Melbourne
Mexico City   Nairobi   Paris   Singapore
Taipei   Tokyo   Toronto

and associated companies in
Berlin   Ibadan

Oxford is a trade mark of Oxford University Press

First published 1992
This impression (lowest digit)
11   13   15   17   19   20   18   16   14   12

Illustrated by K.Y. Chan

Syllabus designer: David Foulds

Text processing and analysis by Luxfield Consultants Ltd

ISBN 0 19 585272 9

Printed in Hong Kong
Published by Oxford University Press (China) Ltd
18/F Warwick House East, Taikoo Place, 979 King's Road,
Quarry Bay, Hong Kong

CONTENTS

THE UNHAPPY KING

The King wants a wife

Long ago, there was a great king called Shahriah. He
was a good king — until he found his wife loved
another man. Then the King was very angry with his
wife. 'Cut off her head!' he roared. The executioner   5
took the King's wife away, and cut her head off.

Every night after that the King lay in his great bed
all alone and very sad. When he slept, he dreamed of
his beautiful, dead wife. When he was awake, he
thought he could see her in the
arms of the other man. He did
not know what to do. At last
he called for the Wazir, the
chief of his servants.

The sleepy Wazir hurried to the King's room.

'I will not spend another night by myself,' said the King.

'Oh, you have decided to marry again. I am so glad, dear King,' cried the Wazir, happily.

'Marry again? How can I do that? Women are so bad. A woman cannot love one man for more than one day.'

A new wife every day

'Any woman would love you for ever, great King,' said the Wazir.

'You are wrong!' roared King Shahriah. 'A woman's love is like a leaf in the wind. One minute it goes this way, the next minute it goes another way. No one ever knows where it will go next.'

'Of course, you are right, O great King,' said the Wazir quickly. 'Women are just like leaves. But what can anyone do?'

'I know what I shall do,' said the King. 'And you are going to help me. Bring me a pretty, clever girl and I will marry her.'

The Wazir looked pleased.

Then the King added, 'And tell the executioner to come to the wedding. He must cut off the girl's head the next morning, before she can stop loving me. After that, you must bring me another girl. As long as you do your job, I shall never be alone at night again. As long as the executioner does his job, no wife of mine will live long enough to love another man!'

The Wazir went away sadly. He hated to send all those lovely girls to their deaths. But he had to obey the King.

The Wazir's daughter

For three years King Shahriah married a new wife every day. Every morning the executioner cut off the head of the King's new wife. More than a thousand girls died.

The Wazir was very unhappy about this, but he was afraid of the King. He was afraid of the executioner, too. He often shut himself in his room and cried. He prayed to God to help him.

One day, someone heard the Wazir crying. That person was the Wazir's daughter. She was beautiful, clever and good, and her name was Sheherezade. The Wazir loved her more than anything in the world.

Sheherezade walked into her father's room.

'Why are you so sad, Father?' she asked.

'Dear child,' said the Wazir, 'I am crying for a thousand lovely young girls. Every day the King marries a new wife. Every morning his executioner cuts off her head.'

'But why?' asked Sheherezade. Her father told her the whole sad story. 'It makes me so sad that it will break my heart,' he finished, 'but I don't know what I can do.'

Sheherezade's plan

Sheherezade was sad, too, when she heard about the poor young girls. She thought carefully for a few minutes. Then she said:

'Listen, Father. I think I know how we can stop the King from killing any more young girls. Let me marry him.'

'You? Oh, my dear daughter, do not throw your

life away! Do not leave your poor old father alone in the world!'

'Father, please do as I ask you. I have a plan.'

King Shahriah was very happy when he saw Sheherezade. 'Why didn't you bring this one to me before, Wazir?' he said.

'She is my own daughter, great King,' said the Wazir, very sadly.

That night Sheherezade lay beside the King in his great bed. She began to tell him a story. Shahriah had never heard a story like it before.

The story was about a place far, far away where people did strange things. Sometimes the story was funny, and the King laughed. He had not laughed so much for many years. Sometimes it was sad, and he could not stop crying. He had not cried so much for many years, either. Always it was interesting. But before Sheherezade reached the end of the story, day had come.

The wonderful stories

The sun was up in a pink sky, and the birds were singing their morning song.

'It is day,' said the King. 'I have work to do. Tonight, Sheherezade, you must come to me again. You can finish the story then.'

The executioner was standing outside the door. 'Not this morning,' the king told him. 'Come again tomorrow.'

So Sheherezade lived one day longer than all the other young girls.

The next night she finished her story. Then she started a new one. This story, too, was about a wonderful place far, far away. The King laughed even louder at the funny parts. He cried even longer at the sad parts. He was so interested in the story that before he knew it, it was daytime. And of course, Sheherezade had not finished.

Once again the King sent the executioner away. He asked Sheherezade to come back the next night to finish her second story.

So it went on, night after night, week after week, month after month. Sheherezade knew so many different stories. Each one was new. Each one was too long to finish before day came.

Here are just a few of the stories that she told the King.

THE GENIE IN THE BOTTLE

A bottle of dust

There was once a poor, old fisherman. Every day he
went to the sea with his net. Every day he prayed to
God to fill his net with fish. Sometimes God
5 answered his prayers; often He did not.

One morning the fisherman
pulled his net out of the water.
There was nothing in it except
a dirty, old bottle.

10 The fisherman was sad. He
wanted fish, not an old bottle.

'Perhaps I can sell it,' he said to
himself. He washed the mud off the
bottle and looked at it. It was very

15 old, and it was fastened with a strange
seal. The fisherman did not know
much about old things. He did not
know that the seal on the bottle
was the seal of the great King

20 Solomon himself. 'Perhaps
there is something useful
in the bottle,' he said
to himself. He opened
the bottle with

25 his knife.

He looked inside. The bottle was empty. Then the fisherman turned it over and shook it. Dust came out, at first just a little, then more and more. Faster and faster, dust flew out of the bottle and up into the air like a dark cloud. The cloud grew and grew. Soon the 5 fisherman saw the shape of a huge man of dust. It was a magic man, a genie.

An angry genie

Some genies are small and friendly, but this one was as tall as a mountain and as fierce as a tiger. It did not 10 look at all friendly. It looked angry, and bad.

The fisherman's mouth hung open. His eyes were as big as plates, and he was very frightened. He knelt on the sand and prayed to God to save him. When the genie spoke, the earth shook and the sky grew 15 dark.

'Oh Solomon, great king. I am sorry, and I will never do it again — ' The genie stopped and looked at the frightened little fisherman. 'You are not Solomon!' 20

The fisherman shook his head. He said nothing. He was too frightened to speak.

'Who let me out of the bottle?' asked the genie.

'I did, sir,' said the fisherman.

'Get ready to die, little man,' roared the genie. 25

'But what have I done to you, Great One?'

'Choose the way you want to die, little man,' said the genie. 'Make it painful and nasty and very horrible. If it is not horrible enough I will think of a much more horrible way.' 30

'But what have I done?' repeated the poor fisherman. 'How have I made you so angry?'

'Listen, little man, I will tell you my story — but get ready to die afterwards. Don't think I will forget.'

The genie's tale

'I am a great genie,' said the genie, 'and I fought against King Solomon himself. My army was beaten and King Solomon made me his prisoner. I knelt down and begged him for my life. He could see how sorry I was.

'"Stand up," King Solomon said to me. "Just obey me. Then I shall forgive you, and we can be friends."

'"You forgive me?" I roared. "Me! I am the greatest, strongest genie in the whole world. You will have to wait a long time before I will do as you tell me! And you will wait much, much longer before I will become your friend!"

'Then King Solomon said some magic words, and I suddenly felt myself getting smaller and smaller. He put me in this bottle. He closed it up with his own great seal. Then he told one of his soldiers to throw it into the sea. That's my story,' said the genie.

'But King Solomon died two thousand years ago!' said the fisherman.

'Two thousand years!' cried the genie. 'So my old enemy is dead and I cannot kill him! Well, little man, you can take his place. I shall kill you, instead. Get ready to die.' He took a long, shining knife out of his belt, and he smiled a big, ugly smile.

The simple fisherman

The genie looked down at the fisherman. He thought the little man would be very frightened. But the fisherman was looking at the genie with a smile on his tired, old face.

'Well, now,' said the fisherman, 'you don't think I am going to believe that, do you?'

'You don't believe me?' roared the genie. He was so angry that the sea and the sky shook. He lifted the big knife above his head. But the fisherman just smiled again.

'Now, tell me the truth — where did you come from? You didn't come out of that little bottle, did you? I know I am a simple man, but I am not stupid. How could a great genie get inside such a small bottle?'

'I am a genie,' said the genie. 'Genies can do anything!'

'Well I am not going to believe that,' said the fisherman. 'Look — I am a lot smaller than you, and I can't get into that bottle.' He tried to push his foot down through the neck of the bottle, and of course he could not do it. 'You can't tell me,' the fisherman continued, 'that you and that big shining knife got inside this tiny little bottle. It's just silly.'

The genie was so angry. 'Me?' he roared. 'Silly?' he roared. 'You are the silly one, little man. Can't you understand? A great genie like me can do anything. Watch!'

5   **Back in the bottle**

The body of the genie, tall as a mountain, broke up into a cloud of many different colours. The cloud grew smaller and smaller. At last, all that was left was some dust. The dust went through the neck of the
10   bottle.

'Oh!' smiled the old fisherman. 'So that's how you do it! Now I know you are a great genie.' Then he quickly took the seal and pushed it on top of the bottle. The bottle was fastened again — and the genie
15   was inside!

'And you can stay there for another two thousand years!' cried the fisherman. 'I shall tell the people in my village about you, too! Then, if they find your bottle, they will know they must not let you out.'

20   He thanked God for His help and he threw the bottle far away into the sea.

ALADDIN AND THE
MAGIC LAMP

The strange uncle

There was once a tailor called Mustapha. Every day,
he worked very hard. He worked from morning to
night, but he was always very poor. His son, Aladdin,
was a lazy boy and did nothing to help him. Then   5
Mustapha died. After that Aladdin was much more
lazy. His poor mother had to work to buy food for
them.

One day, Aladdin was playing in the street when a
stranger came up to him. 'Boy,' said the stranger, 'are   10
you the son of Mustapha the tailor?'
'Yes,' answered Aladdin, 'but my father is dead.'

The stranger looked very sad. He threw his arms
round Aladdin's neck. 'I am your uncle, dear boy,' he
said. 'I have been away for many years. Now I   15
am too late to see my poor,
dear brother!' He took some
money out of his pocket
and gave it to Aladdin.

'Go to your mother and tell her I have returned. Tell her I will visit her tomorrow.'

A job for Aladdin

Aladdin ran home and told his story. 'But your father had no brothers!' said his mother. 'You must have made a mistake. I will tell the kind gentleman when he comes.'

The next evening the stranger came. He held Aladdin's mother's hands. 'So I am too late to see my dear brother!' he said. He looked so sad. Aladdin's mother began to cry.

Now, the stranger was not really Aladdin's uncle. He was a magician. He wanted Aladdin to help him. But he did not say anything about that to Aladdin. Instead, he looked at the boy and asked, 'What job have you chosen to do, nephew?' Aladdin went very pink. 'Nothing,' he said.

'Then I shall buy you a shop,' said the magician. 'Say goodbye to your mother. You are going to learn all about business. I will do everything I can to help you. Only the best is good enough for my dear brother Mustapha's boy.'

Aladdin's mother was now sure the magician was Aladdin's uncle. She thanked him with all her heart. 'Be good, and work hard, Aladdin,' she told her son.

The magic halls

The magician led Aladdin to a place outside the city. He told Aladdin to collect sticks for a fire. When the fire was burning, the magician threw some white dust on to the fire. Then he said some magic words.

Green smoke rose up. The earth shook, and a large hole suddenly opened in front of them. At the bottom of the hole, Aladdin saw a big, flat stone with an iron ring in the middle.

'Take the ring in your hand and lift the stone,' 5 said the magician. Aladdin was frightened. 'Do as I tell you,' the magician said. 'There is a wonderful treasure down there. Only you can reach it. Your name is written on the stone.'

Aladdin lifted the stone. It moved quite easily. 10 Under the stone were some steps. They went down into the ground. Aladdin could see that it was very dark down there.

'Go down those steps,' said the magician. 'At the bottom you will come to a large hall. It is full of 15 boxes of gold and silver. Do not touch anything. Keep walking. You will come to another hall. Go through that one, and you will come to a third hall. At the end of this hall, there is a door. Open the door. You will see a garden full of beautiful fruit trees. In 20 a corner of the garden wall there is a shelf. On the shelf you will see a small lamp. Bring that lamp to me. You can take some of the treasure when you come back if you like. But do not forget the lamp.'

Aladdin goes down the steps   25

Aladdin was frightened. He did not want to go down those dark steps. The magician put a ring on Aladdin's finger. 'This is a magic ring, and it will keep you safe,' he said.

Aladdin thanked him and went down the steps. 30 Everything was just as the magician had said. He found the lamp and put it in his pocket. On his way

back he looked at the
trees full of beautiful fruit.
When he tried to eat the fruit, it was
hard and cold. Aladdin did not know
5 that the wonderful pears, oranges and
apples were huge jewels. He just thought
they were pretty, and he filled his pockets with them.

The magician was waiting at the top of the steps.
He planned to get the lamp, then shut the door, with
10 Aladdin inside.

'Help me up, Uncle,' called Aladdin.

'Give me the lamp first,' said the magician. 'You
will climb up better without it.'

'It's in my pocket,' called Aladdin, 'under some
15 pretty fruit. I'll give it to you when I get out.'

Alone in the dark

The magician was angry.

'Do as I tell you. Give the lamp to me,' he said.

'I can't, Uncle,' said Aladdin. 'Help me get out of

this hole. When I am out I will take everything out of my pockets. Then you can have the lamp.'

But the magician did not want to wait. He was very angry. He threw some more dust on the fire. He said some more magic words. This time, red smoke rose up into the air. There was a loud, frightening noise. The big stone slid back, and the earth closed over the hole. Aladdin was a prisoner in the earth! The angry magician went away.

Aladdin cried for help, but no one heard him. After a while he was tired and stopped shouting. His hands began to feel cold, so he rubbed them together. Suddenly a small genie appeared.

'I am the Genie of the Ring,' it said. 'What can I do for you?' Aladdin was too surprised to be frightened.

'Please get me out of here!' he answered. At once he found himself sitting on the grass outside.

The Genie of the Lamp

He ran home to his mother and showed her the pretty fruit.

'Why didn't you bring some of the gold and silver?' said his mother. 'You are a stupid boy! There is no food in the house, and we can't eat your glass fruit.'

'I brought this lamp,' said Aladdin. 'If you clean it, perhaps I can sell it in the market.'

He began to rub the lamp. A cloud of smoke flew out and a large genie appeared.

'I am the Genie of the Lamp,' it said. 'What can I do for you?'

'Bring some food,' said Aladdin. The genie disappeared. In a few seconds it came back with a big, silver dish full of wonderful food.

'This must be a magic lamp, Mother,' said Aladdin.
'Now I know why my uncle wanted it so much! He
must be a magician.'

Every day after that, the Genie of the Lamp brought
5 them food on a silver dish, and every day Aladdin sold
the silver dish in the market. He did not know the
price of silver, so the shopkeepers gave
him very little money. But
Aladdin and his mother were
10 poor, simple people, and
they were happy with
what they had.

ALADDIN AND THE PRINCESS

Princess Badroulbadour

One day, Aladdin went to the market as usual, to sell the genie's silver dish. This time, he went to a different shopkeeper. He gave Aladdin a lot of money for the dish. Aladdin showed him some of the fruit $_5$ from the magic trees.

'I'm sure that you won't want these,' he said. 'But aren't they beautiful?'

'They are wonderful jewels,' said the shopkeeper. 'Take care of them, my boy. They are great treasures.' $_{10}$

Suddenly there was a lot of noise in the street. 'What is happening?' asked Aladdin.

'Princess Badroulbadour is coming this way,' said the shopkeeper. 'She is the King's daughter. She comes past here on her way to the baths. $_{15}$ The King will not let anyone see her face, so everyone has to go inside.'

Aladdin wanted to see her. He hid behind a wall near the baths. Soon Princess Badroulbadour $_{20}$ appeared with her servants.

When she came near the door of the baths, she took off her veil. Aladdin saw her lovely face and fell in love with her at once. He went home to his mother. He was quiet all evening.

5   At last he told his mother. 'I love Princess Badroulbadour. I want to marry her,' he said. 'Please go to the King and tell him.'

'You silly boy — do you think the King will let a poor tailor's son marry his daughter?' his mother
10 replied.

'I love her, Mother. I must try to win her. A shop-keeper told me these fruits are wonderful treasures. Put them in one of the silver dishes, and take them to the King. I am sure he will listen to you.'

A present for the King
15

The next day Aladdin's mother took the beautiful silver dish, full of magic fruits, to the King's palace. She put a clean cloth over the dish and waited outside. Soon the King came out and Aladdin's
20 mother called to him.

The King saw the old lady in her poor, thin clothes. He spoke to his Wazir, the chief of his servants. 'Bring that woman here. Perhaps she has a home-made cake for me under that cloth.'

25   Aladdin's mother knelt at the King's feet. 'Forgive me, Great King,' she begged. And then she told him how her son Aladdin loved the Princess Badroulbadour. 'My son sends you these,' she said. She lifted the cloth and the King saw the wonderful
30 jewels. His eyes shone. 'Look, Wazir! Have you ever seen jewels like these? Of course this young man must marry my daughter!'

The Wazir was unhappy. He wanted his son to marry Princess Badroulbadour. 'Give me three months, Great King,' he begged. 'In that time my son will be able to give you a much richer present than this!' 5

The King liked his Wazir, so he agreed. He said to Aladdin's mother, 'Tell your son that I thank him for this wonderful present. Perhaps I will let him marry the Princess Badroulbadour. But he must wait for three months. Then I will decide.' 10

The genie helps Aladdin

Time went by very slowly for Aladdin. Two months passed, then Aladdin heard some horrible news. Princess Badroulbadour was going to marry the Wazir's son that night! Aladdin was hurt and angry. 15 He rubbed the magic lamp and the genie appeared.

'The King has given his daughter to another man,' said Aladdin. 'Bring Princess Badroulbadour and the Wazir's son to me tonight!' The genie disappeared, and returned with Princess Badroulbadour in one 20 hand and the Wazir's son in the other. 'Put him in a safe place,' said Aladdin to the genie. He looked at Badroulbadour.

'Do not be afraid,' he said. 'You are quite safe here. The King said I could marry you, and now he has 25 given you to another man. I had to stop the wedding. Sleep now, and in the morning I will take you back to your father.'

When Badroulbadour saw Aladdin, she fell in love with him. She did not like the Wazir's son. She 30 thought Aladdin would be a much better husband for her.

In the morning the genie took Badroulbadour back
to her room in the King's palace. He took the Wazir's
son back to his father's house.

The frightened young man went to the King at
once. He told him all about the genie. He told him
how the genie had carried him away in one hand,
and the Princess in the other. He thought the Princess
had told the genie what to do. He thought she was a
witch.

'I cannot marry your daughter after all,' said the
Wazir's son.

Badroulbadour said nothing at all. She was
thinking about Aladdin.

The King did not believe the young man's story. He
thought he was mad. He was glad that the Wazir's son
was not going to marry his daughter.

A month later he told his servants to bring
Aladdin's mother to him. 'Your son may marry my
daughter,' he said. 'But first he must bring me forty
gold dishes full of those fruit-jewels.'

Forty dishes full of jewels

'This will teach Aladdin not to be so silly,' the old lady
said to herself. But to her surprise, Aladdin was quite
happy. He went to his room and rubbed the lamp.
The genie appeared at once, and Aladdin told him
what he wanted.

In a very short time the genie came back with forty
servants. Each carried a very large, gold dish. Each
dish was full of the wonderful fruit-jewels from the
magic garden. Aladdin called his mother. 'Go with
these to the King,' he said, 'and tell him I love his
daughter more than all the jewels in the world.'

At first the King was too surprised to speak. He looked at the gold, the jewels and the servants, and his eyes grew large and round. At last he said, 'Tell Aladdin to come at once, and I will welcome him as my son.'

Aladdin went to his wedding like a King. His clothes were covered with jewels and fifty servants followed him. He rode a beautiful black horse, and the servants threw gold coins to all the people. The people shouted and cheered, and the King was very glad. When Aladdin saw the King he asked for some land near the palace.

'I shall build a house for myself and my new wife,' he said. When the king woke up next morning, he looked out of his window. He saw a wonderful palace. It shone with gold and jewels, and all around it were gardens full of beautiful flowers. Of course, this was the work of the Genie of the Lamp, but the King did not know that.

New lamps for old

The wedding was a wonderful day for everyone, except the Wazir. At last the feast was over and Aladdin and Badroulbadour were alone together. He took her in his arms. 'I am the luckiest man in the world,' he said.

The news of Aladdin, his wonderful palace and his lovely wife, reached the magician. He was very angry. He realized that Aladdin was not dead after all. 'So he escaped,' said the magician. 'I must get that lamp.'

He put on his oldest clothes and bought a lot of cheap new lamps. Then he went through the streets calling, 'New lamps for old! Bring me your old lamp, and I will give you a new one!' Many people did this, and at last the news reached Princess Badroulbadour.

Aladdin was not at home, and she wanted to surprise him. She thought he would like to have a nice new lamp. She sent a servant with Aladdin's old lamp. 'He will be so pleased,' she said to herself.

The magician was very pleased. As soon as the servant gave him the old lamp, he rubbed it. The genie appeared. 'Take Aladdin's palace and everyone in it, and put it down in the middle of Africa,' the magician said. The genie picked the palace up in his hands and flew away.

The Genie of the Ring

When Aladdin came home he rubbed his eyes. Where was his beautiful palace? The King looked out of his window and rubbed his eyes too. Where was his beautiful daughter?

The Wazir came up to him. 'I told you not to let your daughter marry that stranger,' he said. 'Now you know all about him. He is a magician, and he has taken your daughter away for ever.'

The King sent his soldiers to get Aladdin. They threw him into prison. The King sent for his executioner. 'Cut off his head!' said the Wazir. 'That will not bring my daughter back,' said the king sadly.

Aladdin began to understand. 'The magician came to the palace while I was out,' he said to himself. 'He found the lamp. That is the only answer.'

Suddenly he remembered the magic ring. He rubbed it and the small genie appeared. 'Genie,' he said, 'go and find my palace and my wife. Bring them back to me at once.'

The genie looked sad. 'I am very sorry, sir,' it said. 'I am not strong enough for that. The Genie of the Lamp is much stronger than I am; you will have to ask him.'

In Aladdin's palace

Aladdin thought for a minute. Then he asked, 'Can you carry me to my palace?' The genie smiled. 'I am sure I can do that, sir,' it said. And it did.

Soon Aladdin was in his own bedroom at the palace. He took the Princess in his arms.

'I've done something wrong,' said Badroulbadour. She told Aladdin about the old man and the lamps. 'He gave me this new one,' she said, 'and he put the old one in his pocket. Then the whole palace flew through the air — I can't understand it.'

'Where is the old man now?' asked Aladdin.

'He is downstairs,' said Badroulbadour. 'He wants to marry me. He says I must decide today.'

'Send for him,' said Aladdin. 'Tell him you agree. But give him some medicine to make him sleep. While he is sleeping, we can take the lamp.' Then Aladdin hid himself in the cupboard in the bedroom.

The story ends happily

Badroulbadour made a lovely cool drink for the magician. Then she sent a servant to invite him to her room. There she took off her veil and showed him her beautiful face. 'Sit down,' she invited him, 'and drink.' The magician drank. Soon he was asleep.

Quickly Badroulbadour took the lamp. Aladdin came out of the cupboard. He took the lamp to his own room, and rubbed it.

'I am glad to see you again, sir,' said the genie. 'What can I do for you?'

A few seconds later, the King looked out of his window and saw Aladdin's palace again, with its lovely gardens. 'I was dreaming,' the King said to himself. Then he remembered Aladdin and the executioner. 'I hope it is not too late!' he said.

Just then Aladdin came into the room with Badroulbadour by his side. The King took them both in his arms. The Wazir stole a horse and quietly rode away from the King's palace.

And so Aladdin and his beautiful wife enjoyed a long and happy life. The bad old magician was left alone in Africa; perhaps he is still there today!

ALI BABA

The magic cave

Once, a long time ago, there were two brothers.
Kassim was rich and greedy. His brother, Ali Baba,
was a kind man. He worked very hard, but he was
poor.   5

Every day Ali Baba went to the forest with his
donkeys. There he cut wood which he sold in the
market.

One day Ali Baba was cutting wood when he saw
a big cloud of dust in front of him. It came closer   10
to where he was. Then he heard the noise of many
horses. Some people were coming.

Ali Baba was a little frightened. He hid his donkeys
behind a big rock. Then he climbed up into a tree.
The tree had big leaves, and no one could see him   15
there.

Ali Baba looked through the leaves. He saw forty
men on black horses. They stopped just under the
tree, but they did not look up. They looked at a big
wall of rock a few yards away.   20

'Open Sesame!' called the leader of the men. The
wall of rock opened wide and Ali Baba saw a large,
dark cave. The men took some heavy bags off their
horses and carried them into the cave. The bags were
full of gold, silver and jewels.   25

'These men are thieves,' said Ali Baba to himself.
'They are hiding the things they have stolen in this
magic cave.' He saw the robbers come out again.

They climbed on their horses. The chief shouted
'Close Sesame!' and the door of the cave shut. Then
they all rode away.

Ali Baba is rich

5 When the air was still and quiet again, Ali Baba
climbed down from his tree. He stood
in front of the wall of rock and
shouted, 'Open Sesame.' At once
the cave door opened and Ali
10 Baba went inside.

The cave was full of
treasure. Ali Baba took a
small bag of gold. It was almost
too heavy for him to move, but he
15 got it outside at last. 'Close Sesame!' he
said, and the cave doors closed. Then he
put his treasure on the back of one of his donkeys.
He put some wood on top, then he went home.

His wife was very excited and she began to count
the gold. There was so much! She got as far as a
hundred pieces, then she forgot, and had to start

again. 'I can't count all this gold,' she said to her
husband.

'There is enough to make us rich,' said Ali Baba.
'Why do you want to count it?'

But his wife was unhappy. She wanted to know   5
just how rich she was. She went to Kassim's wife
and asked her for her scales.

Kassim's wife said to herself,
'Why does Ali Baba's wife want
my scales?' She always wanted
to know all about everything.
Before she gave the scales
to Ali Baba's wife, she
rubbed a little fat on them.

Ali Baba's wife ran home
and weighed the gold coins.
Then she gave the scales back
to Kassim's wife. She did not notice that one small
gold coin was stuck to the bottom of the scales.

A greedy man   20

Kassim's wife showed the coin to her husband. 'I
thought your brother was a poor man!' she cried.
'But now his wife has so much gold that she has to
weigh it!' Kassim was angry. He went to Ali Baba's
house to talk to him.   25

'Where did you get your gold, brother?' he asked
Ali Baba. Ali Baba had to tell him the story of the
thieves and the cave.

Kassim wanted all the treasure for himself. For
days he followed Ali Baba into the forest. At last Ali   30
Baba went to the cave to get another small bag
of gold. Kassim hid behind a rock and watched.

'Open Sesame,' said Ali Baba, and the door of the cave opened. 'I must remember those words,' said Kassim to himself.

5 Next day Kassim went to the wall of rock and said, 'Open says-a-me.' The cave door opened and Kassim ran inside. 'Close says-a-me!' he called. He did not want to leave the door open. He wanted to be in the cave a long time. He wanted to look at all the wonderful gold and silver and jewels.

10 He picked up a large bag and slowly filled it with lovely things. At last, when the bag was full, he went back to the cave door.

'Open says me!' he shouted. Nothing happened. 'Open me says!' said Kassim. Still nothing happened.
15 Poor Kassim had forgotten the magic word. He could not get out. For hours and hours he tried again and again.

Kassim's body

Then the door opened, but not because of Kassim. The
20 thieves had come. They had opened the cave door from the outside. They were bringing more treasure.

When the robbers came into the cave, they saw Kassim. They were cruel men. They took out their knives and killed him. They cut his body into small
25 pieces. Then they went away again.

Night came, and Kassim did not come home for dinner. His wife went to Ali Baba. She told him that Kassim had gone to the magic cave.

Ali Baba thought that his brother was in danger. He
30 hurried to the cave. There he found the pieces of Kassim's body on the floor. Sadly, he collected them together and took them home.

Ali Baba had a good, clever servant girl. Her name was Morgiana and she helped Ali Baba's wife in the house.

When Ali Baba came home he showed her the little pieces of Kassim's body. 'What can we do?' he asked. 'When we bury Kassim everyone will see his body is in pieces. They will all start talking. Then the thieves will hear about it and they will know the man in the cave was Kassim. They will learn that I am his brother. They will come here and kill us all.'

'Leave it to me,' said Morgiana.

The torn coat

Morgiana knew a clever tailor. She covered his eyes and she led him at night to Ali Baba's house. There, in a dark room, the tailor sewed the body together.

'No one will know that Kassim was the person in the cave,' said Ali Baba to himself. 'Kassim had an accident in the forest,' he told Kassim's wife.

They buried the body next morning. No one asked them any questions.

When the thieves went back to the cave, the body was gone!

'Someone came into the cave while we were away,' said the chief of the thieves. 'That means someone knows the magic words. We must find him and kill him.'

The thieves asked a lot of questions in the town. 'Did anyone bury a body that was cut into pieces?' they asked. No one knew anything.

Then one day the chief tore his coat. He took it to a tailor and asked him to mend it. He watched the tailor doing his work. He was using only a very small, weak lamp.

'How can you sew with so little light?' asked the chief.

5   'I don't need much light,' explained the tailor. 'I use my fingers, not my eyes. I can sew with my eyes shut. Last week I sewed a man's body together in the dark!' He told the chief all about the body in Ali Baba's house. 'Lead me there,' said the chief. He gave the tailor a gold coin and covered his eyes with a cloth. The tailor led him to Ali Baba's house. The chief took a piece of white chalk out of his pocket and marked a large cross on the door.

'Tomorrow,' said the chief to his men, 'we will burn down that house — and we will kill our enemy too.'

25   **Morgiana saves everyone**

Early next morning Morgiana went outside to do some work. She saw the white chalk cross. She did not know what it meant, but she did not like it. She got another piece of chalk. She marked a large white
30   cross on every door in the street.

When the thieves arrived, they did not know what to do. Their chief went back to the tailor. Again he paid the tailor to lead him to Ali Baba's house. This time he was sure.

'Listen to my plan,' he told his men. 'I shall pretend that I am selling oil. We'll get twenty donkeys and forty oil jars. Each of you must hide in one of the jars. When it is time, I will lift up the lids. Then you must jump out and kill everyone.'

The forty oil jars

The thirty-nine thieves hid in the oil jars. Their chief filled the fortieth jar with oil. That evening he knocked at Ali Baba's door.

'Good friend,' he said, 'my twenty donkeys and I have nowhere to stay. If I give you this jar of oil, will you let us sleep in your yard?'

'Keep your oil, my friend,' said Ali Baba. 'You are welcome. Give water to your donkeys, then come and eat with us.'

Morgiana was cooking the dinner. She needed more oil and the shops were already shut. 'There are forty jars of oil in the yard,' she said to herself. 'No one will know if I take a little.'

She took a jug and went into the yard. She opened the nearest jar. 'Is it time?' said a man's voice.

Morgiana was very surprised. At first she thought it was a genie. But she was brave as well as clever. 'No,' she said to the robber in the jar. She went to the next jar, and the next. The same thing happened. At last she found the one jar that contained oil.

Morgiana took her jug of oil into the kitchen. 'Good men do not hide in oil jars,' she said to herself. 'They are going to do something bad. And I am going to do something to stop them!'

She took her biggest pot from the kitchen and filled it with oil from the jar in the yard. She put the pot of oil on the kitchen fire until the oil was boiling. Carefully she carried it out into the yard. Carefully she
5   opened every jar, and poured very hot oil in. Then she went back to the kitchen and finished cooking the dinner.

The thieves are dead

When everyone was in bed the chief went out into
10   the yard. He lifted the lid of the first jar. 'It is time,' he said. There was no answer. The same thing happened the next time, and the time after that. All his thirty-nine men were dead.

The next morning Ali
15   Baba's guest was gone. He seemed to be in a great hurry. He did not thank Ali Baba for his kind welcome
20   and good dinner. He just rode away with his twenty donkeys and his forty jars. Ali Baba and his wife felt hurt and sad. Only
25   Morgiana understood.

Later she told Ali Baba her story. 'You have saved our lives,' said Ali Baba. 'You are not my servant any more. From today you are my dear
30   daughter.' Ali Baba's wife was very pleased, and so was his son. Morgiana was pretty as well as clever, and the young man fell in love with her.

For a whole year they all lived together in peace. But one day the chief came back. This time he wore the clothes and jewels of a rich man. He pretended to be ill outside Ali Baba's house. Of course, Ali Baba invited him in.

That night Morgiana cooked a wonderful dinner. The stranger saw her pretty face and ate her good food. At once he told Ali Baba that he would pay a good price for her.

'I cannot sell Morgiana,' said Ali Baba. 'Morgiana is like a daughter to me.'

'Then let her be my wife,' said the stranger. Ali Baba's son gave him a black, angry look. Ali Baba was very unhappy. No one likes to say 'No' to a guest.

Morgiana's dance of death

'Would you like to marry me, my little sugar-cake?' said the stranger. Morgiana pretended she was pleased, but her eyes were hard and cold. The stranger tried to take her in his arms. As he did so, his coat opened. Morgiana's quick eyes saw a long knife in his belt.

'Let me dance for you,' she said to the stranger. She went to her room and put on a beautiful dress and a veil of many colours. She carried a little silver drum in one hand and a small knife in the other.

Morgiana danced like a leaf in the wind. As she danced she beat the drum and waved the knife above her head. She danced round and round, faster and faster. The rich stranger tried to catch her; he wanted to hold her beautiful body in his arms.

Suddenly Morgiana threw herself at the stranger. She buried the knife in his heart.

'What have you done?' cried Ali Baba.

'It is the chief of those thieves, Father,' said Morgiana. She opened the dead man's coat and showed Ali Baba the knife.

Safe at last

'Now we can live in peace at last!' said Ali Baba. 'And Morgiana saved us all.' Soon Morgiana married Ali Baba's son; it was a happy wedding. For a long time they lived together in peace.

After a year Ali Baba felt brave enough to go back to the magic cave. Long grass and tall plants covered the wall of rock. But when Ali Baba said 'Open Sesame' the cave opened as easily as before. All that treasure was Ali Baba's.

Ali Baba became the richest man in the city. No one was unhappy with him because he was never greedy. He built a lovely house for his wife and himself. He bought a farm for his son and Morgiana. He also gave a lot of money to the poor people. Every night he knelt down beside his bed and thanked God for his good luck.

THE TALE OF SINBAD
THE SAILOR

We sail away

When I was still quite young, my father died and left
me all his money. I bought a ship. I paid a captain
and some sailors to work for me. I was sure I was
going to make a lot of money.   5

We sailed far away across the
sea. At last we saw a small island.
It wasn't very big: just a yellow
beach and a few small plants.
Some of us decided to go on   10
land. The captain was asleep.
We did not wake him. Two of
our sailors took a big wooden
barrel full of dirty clothes.
'Perhaps there is fresh water   15
on this island,' they said. 'It will
be good to wash our clothes in fresh water again!'
  We lit a fire on the beach. Suddenly we saw some
water shooting up into the air. It flew up, higher than
the tallest tree, then it dropped down again. I closed   20
my eyes and rubbed them. When I opened them
again I could not believe what I saw.

The island comes to life

Suddenly we heard the voice of the captain. He was
awake now, and he could see what was happening.   25

'Come back to the ship!' he shouted. 'You are in horrible danger!'

'The island is moving!' the sailor shouted. We ran to our little boat. The ship was sailing away from us, and the island was going down. Already the yellow beach was smaller.

'We are on a huge fish!' one of the sailors cried. 'Our fire has woken it!'

He was right. That was no island. It was the sleeping body of a huge fish, the largest fish in the world. For years and years it slept; now it was awake, and it was also in pain. Its huge tail flew up into the air and fell on our little boat. The boat broke into a thousand pieces. I was frightened. I thought I was going to die.

Do you know what saved my life? It was that stupid barrel of dirty clothes! I saw it beside me in the water, and I held on to it and climbed in. The sailors went down with the huge fish to the bottom of the sea.

The strange church

The ship was far away. I was alone in the wide, empty sea. I do not know how long I was in my barrel, but at last I woke up on a wide white beach. 'Where am I?' I thought. 'If I climb a tree, perhaps I can see something.'

I climbed a tree and looked around. Far away I saw a huge, shining white dome. 'There must be a church over there!' I cried. I walked very fast on my poor, tired legs, towards the dome.

When I arrived, I found no doors or windows. The whole dome was as white and smooth as an egg. I did not understand it.

Suddenly the sky grew dark. Was it a
rain cloud? I looked up and saw
a huge bird, larger than the
biggest cloud you have ever
seen. It was a great giant of a   5
bird: the largest bird in all
the world. Then I knew
something else — the
church was a bird's egg!

Before I could run away, the
bird flew down and sat on its egg. I was a
prisoner under its great, hot body.
My turban fell off my head.

That made me think of a plan. I
tied myself to the bird's foot with the   15
cloth of my turban. I prayed to God
to help me, and then I went to sleep.

Snakes and diamonds

When I woke, the wind was blowing past my ears.
I was hanging under the bird's foot. There was   20
nothing except empty air between me and the

ground! Every beat of the bird's great wings was carrying me higher. I looked down and saw the egg. It looked as small as a toy. I shut my eyes again and began to pray.

5   Up and up we went. The air grew thin and cold. When I opened my eyes, the bird was flying slowly, very close to the ground. I untied my turban from its foot and jumped down.

I fell into a strange, lonely place. There were black
10   rocks everywhere: no trees, no grass, no water. I cried to God, 'Oh, Father, why did you save me from the sea? Was that death too gentle for me?'

I looked round. There were great walls of rock all around me. They were very high and there was
15   nowhere to climb up. I was sure I could never get out.

Suddenly something moved beside a rock. It was a snake. I saw many more snakes asleep on the hot rocks. One of them woke and began to move towards me. I picked up a stone to throw at it. Then I looked
20   at the stone, and my mouth fell open with surprise. It was a huge, beautiful diamond: bigger than the biggest diamond you have ever seen! Everywhere I looked the ground was covered with diamonds and other jewels. 'What a place!' I said to myself.
25   'Snakes — and diamonds!'

Just then a large bird flew down and caught one of the snakes. The others moved away. They were frightened of birds.

Saved by a piece of meat

30   Just then something heavy fell down on the ground beside me. At first I thought it was one of the big birds, then I realized it was a piece of meat.

Later I understood what was happening. The people who live in that place want the diamonds, but they are afraid of the snakes. They throw large pieces of meat down. Some of the diamonds stick to the meat. When the large birds come, they carry the meat and the diamonds out of that horrible place.

I saw a way to escape. I filled my pockets with diamonds, then I took the piece of meat in both hands, and held it up. One of the birds flew down to get the meat. It lifted the piece of meat — and me — off the ground and flew towards its nest. Its baby was waiting (that baby was as big as a sheep). The bird began to tear up the meat to give to its baby. I thought it would tear me up and give me to the baby, too.

A new friend

Suddenly I heard shouts. Stones flew into the nest. The bird dropped the meat and flew away. A face looked at me over the edge of the nest.

Now you know how the people get the diamonds. Brave (or greedy) men climb up to the birds' nests. They frighten the birds away and take the jewels. Some people will do anything for money!

'There are no diamonds in this nest, my friend,' I said to the man. He was too surprised to answer. 'Forgive me,' I went on. 'I do not want to frighten you. Just help me to get out of here! I have many beautiful diamonds in my pockets. I shall be glad to give you half of them.'

That man was a true friend to me. He helped me down from the bird's nest. He gave me clean clothes and good food. He helped me to sell my jewels. I had enough money to buy six beautiful ships.

I wanted to sail to Baghdad, but we were a long way from home. No one knew of such a place. I found captains for my ships and filled them with treasure. I sent them to all the four corners of the world to look for Baghdad. I was sure that, one day, they must hear news of my home. I myself got into the biggest treasure ship of all. We sailed with the wind. 'God makes the wind blow,' I said, 'I hope He will send me home.'

Monkey-sailors

One morning we saw an island. 'Fresh water at last,' I said. The captain shook his head. 'I don't think I like this place,' he said.

Suddenly a small ship came towards us at top speed. Its sailors were as small as monkeys. There were hundreds of them and they came onto our ship and fought with us.

Soon we were all prisoners on our own ship. The little monkey-men sailed our ship to the island. Its name was Zugb — an ugly name for an ugly place. They picked us up — five of them could carry one of our sailors easily — and took us to the beach. There they left us. Then they got into my lovely ship and sailed away.

'Well,' I said to the captain, 'we have lost our ship and our treasure, but we still have our lives.' The captain did not answer. He was praying.

I looked round. Behind the beach was a very large house with a very high wall all round it. The great iron gate was open, so we went inside.

We looked for somewhere to sleep. We saw no one, but there were white bones on the ground. 'Are they for the dogs?' I said. The captain went very white and said nothing.

The hungry giant

Soon we heard a noise like thunder. A huge, ugly man came through the gates. He was bigger than an elephant, and much uglier. He was a great giant: the tallest, fattest, ugliest, hungriest giant in the world! He locked the gates behind him with a large key.

The giant lit a fire in the yard outside his house. He sat down beside it, and looked at us. He was not surprised to see us. Suddenly I realized: the 'monkeys' often brought poor sailors to him. Now I knew where the bones came from.

He picked me up in one hand and felt
my arms and legs.

'Too thin,' he shouted. He picked up
our fattest sailor. That poor man was our
5   cook. The giant cooked him. He put him
on a long metal stick and held him over
the fire. Then he ate the poor man.
After his meal the giant fell asleep.

This went on for many days. The
10   giant gave us food and water; he wanted
us to be fat. Every morning he went out
and locked his gates behind him. Every
evening he ate one of us for supper.

A plan of escape

15   I thought of a plan. 'We must make a
ladder,' I said, 'and escape over the wall.'
We used benches from the giant's
kitchen. 'Later, if we are lucky,' I said,
'we can use them as a boat.' The benches
20   made a good, long ladder.

That night the giant fell asleep after his supper, and
I began the other half of my plan. I got two long
metal sticks. (You will remember, the giant cooked
his food on them). We put them in the fire until they
25   were white-hot. Then two of us ran with the white-
hot sticks and pushed them into the giant's eyes.

He roared with pain and jumped up. Of course, he
was blind, but he could still hear us. 'Quick!' I called.
'Over the wall!' We climbed the ladder. Then we
30   pulled it over the wall and threw it into the sea. This
was our boat. It was not very good but it was better
than nothing.

We sailed all night. At last the moon went down and the sky in the east grew brighter. I saw something in front of us; it looked like land.

The horrible sea snake

'Wake up!' I called to the sailors. 'I can see land. The   5
sea near the land is quite calm.'

In some parts of the world there are islands like rings of rock around a calm lake. This island looked like that. We sailed towards it. But suddenly the 'island' came to life. No, it was not another fish. It was   10
a huge snake. It was the largest snake in the world. Its great head rose out of the water. Its eyes were hard and cold. It saw us. It opened its mouth, and its great teeth closed down on six poor sailors. The captain fell into the water and I never saw him again.   15
I was alone with this horrible sea snake.

'Well,' I said to myself, 'if I am going to die, I will use these benches to make a coffin.' (In Baghdad, everyone wants to be buried in a wooden coffin.) I untied the benches and made them into a long box   20
with a lid. It looked just like a coffin. I lay in my new coffin and prayed for a quick, easy death.

The sea snake swam round and round my coffin. It tried to get inside and eat me, but it could not. At last it swam away.

Saved again

I do not know how long I spent in my coffin. I was alone on the wide, dangerous sea. At last a ship came past.

'Look,' one of the sailors called to his friends. 'There's a box in the water. Shall we see what's inside?'

They sent a boat to collect the coffin. They were very surprised when they found a man inside! I was more dead than alive. The sailors gave me food and water, then they let me rest. They were good, kind men who asked no questions. For a few days I ate, slept and tried to forget that horrible sea snake.

At last I felt able to talk a little. The sailors were very surprised to hear my story.

'So you are from Baghdad?' they said. 'Our captain is from Baghdad too. He is a strange man. Do you know, he has so much treasure, but he won't spend any of it. He says it belongs to the owner of his ship.'

'Who is that?' I asked.

'A man called Sinbad.'

Back in Baghdad

The sailors told me about Sinbad. 'He disappeared seven years ago,' they said, 'but the captain is still waiting for him. Poor Sinbad! A huge fish ate him. But the captain has never stopped hoping and praying.'

I begged the sailors to take me to their captain. We knew each other at once. He was the very first captain of my very first ship. 'So you kept my treasure safe for me,' I said. 'You must have half of it, and when we get back to Baghdad we will have a feast.'

We had a surprise when we arrived in Baghdad. I found all my ships waiting for me there. You will remember that I sent treasure ships to look for Baghdad? Well, every one arrived there with the treasure. I was as rich as a king. 5

The captain bought himself a beautiful ship and went to sea again. I stayed in Baghdad for a time, then I went to sea again. Many more interesting things happened to me ... but that is enough for one story! 10

THE MAN WITH THREE WIVES

The first wife

Sidi Ahmad was a lucky man. He had a nice home, a pretty wife and a pleasant job. He had a donkey too. Every day he cut wood in the forest and sold it in the
5 market. He was very happy. Only one thing in his life was wrong. Sidi Ahmad's wife never stopped talking.

'Why don't you come home earlier? You never talk to me! You never tell me I'm pretty! I don't know if you love me. Perhaps you don't. You spend all your
10 time in the forest. Do you love the trees more than me?' She went on and on. Sidi Ahmad loved her, but he was always very glad to get into the forest. It was quiet and peaceful there.

But one morning, his wife got on the donkey's
15 back. 'I'm coming with you,' she said. 'I want to make sure you work hard. We never have much money. I'm sure you spend half the day dreaming.'

Sidi Ahmad said nothing. But he thought of a clever plan.

20 When they had gone a little way towards the forest, he stopped the donkey. 'My dear,' he said, 'I wasn't going to tell you. I wanted it to be a surprise. But there is a wonderful treasure down there.'

'Down where? Down in that old well?' said Sidi
25 Ahmad's wife. 'Don't just stand there talking. Take me to the well and let me look!'

'It isn't safe, dear. You wait here. I'll go down and get the treasure.'

'No,' said Sidi Ahmad's wife. 'You will go down and stay there all day long. I will look for the treasure for myself.' She made Sidi Ahmad help her get into the bucket. Then he slowly let her down into the deep, dark well.

The quiet genie

Sidi Ahmad smiled quietly. He climbed on the donkey's back and rode away. 'My wife will be very angry,' he said to himself. 'But I don't care; it's so lovely and quiet without her! I'll come back and help her up later.' He spent a happy, busy day in the forest.

When it was getting dark he went back to the well. He pulled up the bucket, and got ready to hear the angry voice of his wife.

'Saved at last!' said a deep, soft voice. 'Oh, my friend, you have saved me from that horrible woman! How can I thank you, my dear, kind friend?'

Sidi Ahmad was very surprised. He almost let go of the bucket. He had not pulled his wife out of the well, but a large, ugly-looking genie.

'I'm a very quiet person,' said the genie. 'I hate noise. I don't like people talking and laughing all the time. I want to be calm and peaceful. Peaceful and calm. That's what I like to be.'

He looked at Sidi Ahmad with large, sad eyes. 'I've lived at the bottom of this well for hundreds of years, you know. No one has ever disturbed me before. Then suddenly this horrible woman appeared. Talking, talking, talking, talking. I have never heard anyone talk so much. But now you have saved me! What a good, kind friend you are!' Then the genie picked up Sidi Ahmad and the donkey and flew away with them.

'Where are we going?' asked Sidi Ahmad.

'Away from that horrible woman, of course,' said the genie. 'Now tell me, what can I give you? Do you want gold? Jewels? A king's daughter for your wife?'

'I don't want another wife, thank you — one is quite enough!' laughed Sidi Ahmad.

✳ The king's daughter

'Not all women are like that,' said the genie. 'Look at this one; and if you want her, she's yours.'

He put Sidi Ahmad carefully down on the roof of a beautiful palace. 'This palace belongs to the King of China,' said the genie. 'His daughter is down there, in the garden.'

Sidi Ahmad looked down at the beautiful young girl. 'Oh, yes. I would like to marry her,' he said. 'Help me, Genie, please!'

'Very well,' said the genie. 'Listen …' He spoke a few words in Sidi Ahmad's ear.

One minute the King's daughter was picking flowers. The next minute she was lying on the ground. She looked dead. The servants ran to her; her eyes were shut and her face was as white as milk. They called the King's doctor, but he could do nothing.

'I will give anything — anything — to the man who makes her well!' promised the King.

Sidi Ahmad walked into the room. 'I hear that your daughter is ill, Great King,' he said. They led him to her. 'I see,' he said. 'A bad genie has got into your daughter, Great King. This sometimes happens in my country. I must try to make the genie go, but it will not be easy.' He spoke to the white, still girl. 'Come out of there, genie. Can't you see the girl's father is frightened?'

The second wife

'It's nice in here!' a deep soft voice said. 'Nice and peaceful!' The voice seemed to come from the lovely lips of the King's beautiful daughter. The King fell down on his knees. 'Please help her!' he cried.

'Get out!' said Sidi Ahmad again.

'Oh, all right!' said the deep voice. The girl's body shook like a leaf and the genie flew out of her mouth in a cloud of smoke.

'Oh, I've had such a strange dream,' the girl said in her own sweet voice. She sat up and rubbed her eyes. Her father ran to her and took her in his arms.

Soon Sidi Ahmad married the King's daughter.

They had a beautiful wedding and were very happy.
Sidi Ahmad forgot about his other wife. The one he
left in the well.

One day some servants arrived from the King of
India. 'Great King,' they said, 'we hear that you
have a wonderful doctor who can make genies obey
him. Our King's daughter is very ill, and the palace
magician can do nothing. He says that a genie is
inside her, and the genie is too strong for him.'

'Of course my son-in-law will help,' said the King
of China. 'He took a genie out of my daughter when
she was close to death. Sidi Ahmad, go at once and
help these good people.'

The third wife

Sidi Ahmad did not want to go. He was very happy
with his new wife, but he had to obey the King.

The King of India was very glad to see Sidi Ahmad.
'Sir,' he said, 'I will give you anything — anything —
if you can help my daughter.'

'I will do my best,' said Sidi Ahmad. He lifted the
girl's veil — and fell in love. She was tall and dark,
with red lips and hair like a black cloud around her
lovely face. 'Dear lady,' he said, 'I am so sorry I can't
help you.'

To his surprise a deep, soft voice answered, 'Oh!
So they asked you to come!' It was the genie from
the well.

'Come out!' cried Sidi Ahmad in a loud voice.
Quietly he whispered, 'If you don't come out, they
will cut off my head!'

'But I like it here,' said the deep voice. 'It is so
calm, so peaceful.'

'Please!' begged Sidi Ahmad. 'I saved you once.'

'That was a long time ago,' said the genie. 'I'm very happy here. I'm going to stay.'

Then Sidi Ahmad remembered something. He looked behind him.

'Genie,' he said. 'I have brought someone with me. She wants to talk to you.'

'Who?' said the deep voice.

'That nice woman from the well,' replied Sidi Ahmad. 'She says she could not find the treasure at the bottom of the well. She thinks you know where it is. Shall I tell her you're here?'

'Oh, no!' said the deep, soft voice. 'Not that talking woman. Talk, talk, talk, talk, talk. Oh, no! Don't tell her I am here. Tell her I have gone away, and you don't know where I am.'

Then the girl's body began to shake like a leaf. The genie flew out of her mouth like a cloud of black smoke. The girl sat up and rubbed her beautiful dark eyes.

'Good day, dear lady,' said Sidi Ahmad. 'Will you marry me?' Of course, she agreed.

The end of the story

And so Sidi Ahmad became the husband of three wives. One was the daughter of the King of China. One was the daughter of the King of India. Both were sweet and pretty and kind, but Sidi Ahmad loved his first wife best. She always took great care of him, and she never said a word.

You see, when Sidi Ahmad was in India, talking to the genie, he remembered his poor first wife. He went straight back to the well and pulled her up.

The cold well had hurt
her throat. She had lost her
voice and could not say anything
to him. Before she could get her
5   voice back, Sidi Ahmad told his servants to make
wells everywhere. Each well had a bucket of gold,
with his wife's name on it.

'How sweet,' people said. 'Sidi Ahmad loves his
first wife so much!' His wife understood, too. She
10   knew that Sidi Ahmad loved her. When her voice got
better, she stayed quiet. She did not want to be a
prisoner in the well again! Yes, Sidi Ahmad was a
very lucky man.

For a thousand and one nights, Sheherezade told the King her stories. She told one wonderful story after another. Every morning she stopped in the middle of a new story. Every morning the King sent his executioner away. He had to hear the rest of the story, and then the next one, and then the one after that. 5

One day he forgot to tell the executioner to come back again. No more lovely young girls died because of King Shahriah after that. 10·

QUESTIONS AND ACTIVITIES

CHAPTER 1

Put the beginning of each sentence with the right ending.

1 The King's wife loved another man ...
a ... because she wanted to stop him killing any more girls.
2 The King was lonely ...
b ... because he did not want to be left alone in the world.
3 The Wazir was happy ...
c ... because he wanted to hear the end of the story.
4 Sheherezade said she would marry the king ...
d ... so the King told the executioner to cut her head off.
5 The Wazir did not want his daughter to marry the king ...
e ... because he thought the king would be married again.
6 The King told the executioner to come back the next day ...
f ... so he told the Wazir to bring him a pretty girl.

CHAPTER 2

Choose the right words to say what this part of the story is about.

The Genie said his army (1) **won a war against/was beaten by** King Solomon. The King made him his (2) **friend/prisoner**. The Genie begged for (3) **his life/some gold**. King Solomon could see how (4) **happy/sorry** he was.

Then the King told the Genie to (5) **stand up/sit down**. He told the Genie to (6) **obey/fight** him. He said if the genie did that they would be (7) **friends/enemies**. The Genie said he was the (8) **smallest/greatest** genie in the world. He did not want to be (9) **friends with/a servant of** the King.

Then the King said some (10) **magic/funny** words. The Genie got (11) **fatter/smaller**. The King put him in the bottle and closed it with (12) **his seal/some glue**. He threw the bottle into the (13) **river/sea**.

CHAPTER 3

Put the words in each sentence in the right order to say what the story is about.

1	Aladdin found the lamp and ...	[pocket] [put] [his] [in] [it].
2	He put some fruit in his pocket,	[on] [lamp] [of] [top] [the].
3	The magician wanted Aladdin ...	[give] [to] [lamp] [him] [the].
4	He planned to shut the door and ...	[inside] [leave] [hole] [the] [Aladdin].
5	Aladdin asked the magician ...	[help] [up] [first] [to] [him].
6	The magician was angry, and he ...	[not] [to] [did] [wait] [want].
7	He threw some dust on the fire and ...	[more] [some] [said] [words] [magic].
8	The big stone slid back and the ...	[over] [earth] [hole] [closed] [the].

CHAPTER 4

Use each of these words once to say what the story is about: **magician, middle, lamp, genie, rubbed, surprise, clothes, servant, old.**

The magician wanted to get the (1) ____. He put on his oldest (2) ____, and bought some cheap new lamps. He told people he would give them a new lamp for their (3) ____ lamps.

Princess Badroulbadour wanted to (4) ____ Aladdin. She thought he would like a nice new lamp. She sent a (5) ____ with Aladdin's old lamp to the (6) ____.

The magician (7) ____ the lamp. He told the (8) ____ to take Aladdin's palace, and everyone in it, to the (9) ____ of Africa.

CHAPTER 5

Put the answers in the right places. In the centre of the puzzle you will see the two words that Kassim forgot. Use these words: **wonderful**, **treasure**, **gold**, **magic**, **closed**, **pieces**, **jewels**, **coin**, **silver**, **cave**. *The first one has been done for you.*

Kassim's wife showed Kassim the gold (1) ____. Later, Ali Baba told Kassim about the thieves and the (2) ____. Kassim wanted all the (3) ____ for himself. When Ali Baba went to the cave to get a small bag of (4) ____, Kassim followed him.

The next day Kassim went into the cave by himself. He (5) ____ the door behind him. He wanted to look at all the (6) ____ gold and (7) ____ and (8) ____. But when he wanted to get out he could not remember the (9) ____ words. The robbers found him in the cave. They killed him and cut his body into small (10) ____.

CHAPTER 6

The underlined sentences are all in the wrong paragraph. Which paragraph should they go in? Write them out in the right place.

1 A huge, ugly man came through the gates. <u>He was blind, but he could still hear us.</u> He locked the gates and then lit a fire in the yard outside his house.

2 The giant picked up our fattest sailor. <u>He was bigger than an elephant.</u> The giant held him over the fire, and then ate the poor man.

3 The giant gave us food and water. <u>He was our cook.</u> Every evening he came home and ate one of us for supper.

4 One night we pushed white-hot sticks into the giant's eyes. <u>He wanted us to be fat.</u> We climbed up the benches, over the wall, and escaped.

CHAPTER 7

The letters in these words are all mixed up. What should they be? (The first one is 'talking'.)

Sidi Ahmad's wife never stopped (1) **ganklit**. Sidi Ahmad loved her, but he was always glad to get away into the (2) **strofe**, where it was quiet and (3) **upcelafe**. One morning his wife said she was going with him. She wanted to make sure he (4) **drokew** hard and didn't spend half the day (5) **inmegard**.

Sidi Ahmad thought of a (6) **velcre** plan. He told his wife that there was a wonderful (7) **estaurer** down in an old well in the forest. Sidi Ahmad's wife made him let her down into the well. Then Sidi Ahmed got on his (8) **yenkod** and rode away.

Later, when it was getting dark, Sidi Ahmad went back and pulled up the (9) **kubect**. He thought he would hear the angry (10) **ocive** of his wife, but he was very (11) **durripess**. Instead of his wife, he pulled up an ugly-looking (12) **inege**.

Oxford
Progressive
English Readers